Find out more about the author and upcoming books online at:
https://linktr.ee/Carrie_Weston

Other books by Carrie Weston

The Xander Chase Series (YA crime fiction/ fantasy)

1. Xander Chase and the Unicorn Code
2. Xander Chase and the Lost Wing
3. Xander Chase and the Battle for Deaths Throne

A Dark Fairy Tale (Fantasy fiction 12+ novella)

0.5 - P.E.T empathiser's PREQUEL (Short Story)

1 - Pet Empathiser Team

2 - Fractured

3. Fabric Of Magic

4. The Fabric Of Magic

Ghost Possessor (YA Paranormal/ fantasy mash)

Ascender

Standalones

An Ampoule of Terror (Horror 18+)

Mistletoe Ball (clean romance part of mistletoe kisses colab)

Frigga (clean romance coming February 2025)

Anthologies

1- Natural Beauty in The Book of Love

2- Cutlemans Rise in The Gift and Other Stories

3- Fallen Elf in Snowflakes & Sleighbells

A Dark Fairy Tale

Pet Empathiser Team

Copyright © Carrie Weston 2021

This novel is a work of fiction. Names, characters, businesses, places, events and incidents are either the products of the author's imagination or used in a fictitious manner. Any resemblance to actual persons, living or dead, or actual events is purely coincidental.

All rights reserved in all media. No part of this publication may be reproduced, stored in a retrieval system, copied in any form or by any means, electronic, mechanical, photocopying, recording or otherwise transmitted without written permission from the author and/or publisher. You must not circulate this book in any format. Any person who does any unauthorised act in relation to this publication may be liable to criminal prosecution and civil claims for damages.

For permission requests, please contact:

authorcarrieweston@gmail.com

Produced in the United Kingdom.

About the author

A bit about me, (OMG — skip this bit quickly). Okay, if you're still checking this out then you want to know something new, so here goes; I love and I *mean* love crystals. I have a huge collection and believe in their properties to aid one's self. As you probably know, I am a divorcee in her early 30's with a young son (who rocks – he did not make me write this) and a crazy springer spaniel who's grumpier than me without coffee (and that's hard). Since I was a kid (and no I don't mean a goat), I've dreamt of becoming a full-fledged authoress.

Thanks for staying tuned

Hearts & Kisses

Follow my blog and sign up for my newsletter with a FREE prequel to this book at;

Carrieweston.co.uk

Or follow me on social media; just click my link tree for all my accounts;

https://linktr.ee/Carrie_Weston

Caroline Hollywell Illustrator

IF YOU'RE LOOKING FOR; MYTHICAL, MAGICAL, WACKY AND WEIRD BOOK COVER ART AND ILLUSTRATIONS THEN CHECK OUT MY GALLERY; Carolinehillustrator (godaddysites.com)

Follow me on;

Facebook – Caroline Hollywell | Facebook

Instagram – Caroline Hollywell

LinkedIn – Caroline Hollywell - Y.A and Children's book Illustrator. - Freelance Illustrator. | LinkedIn

Acknowledgements

Thank you to editor Tiffany Purdon (who has hounded me, along with my son, since the release of the prequel; to find out what happens next) and my Alpha/beta reader (who's very shy; you know who you are).

Hearts and Kisses

Carrie

A message from Jhonathan;

Remember; empathy is what sets us apart.

Prologue

Northan Fae Lands

My name is Jhonathan

I can't tell you where I've been, but you wouldn't believe me. Even now that I'm among my own people, they never stop the hunt for me. The Queen would never allow it.

Not long ago, she enslaved me as her PET. But with the help of the Pet Empathisers and two odd fairy's I escaped through a dragon guarded portal.

Chapter 1

Jhonathan

God, which way is it now? Jhonathan thought as he ran, his ragged trousers flapping about his legs like a whip spurring him on. The streets seemed to have developed their webs of alleys into networks no longer familiar to him. *I don't understand*, he thought. *Everything's different but the same. I just want to go home.* He sprinted as fast as humanly possible, sweat dripping down his body only to be washed away by the pounding rain. He slipped around a corner, bare feet snagging on the gum coated pavement as the, not so missed, repugnant perfume of petrol assaulted his nostrils- resulting in a lung rattling sneeze.

The pain that stabbed at the nerve receptors in his feet didn't bother him as it would have before he was enslaved by the Queen of the fairy's. Her cruelty was unsurpassable. The only thing in his life she couldn't taint with her evil, was the memories of those he loved. Everything else she enjoyed torturing from him with her council of warped Lords and Ladies. Like the kind of sick game, a clowder of cats might play with a wounded mouse. *Come on,* he berated himself. *Concentrate.* Shoving his painful past back into the recess of his mind and focusing on the present and his chance to finally get home and be surrounded by those he loved. Then, there would be time to think on how to defend himself from the Queen's guards and their horrific blood trackers.

Jhonathan's feet throbbed, bloody droplets lay a bread crumb trail as his anguish grew. Heart pounding hard enough for his ribs to protest he swung around a corner, bashing into pedestrians, who scuttled about, desperate to escape in the thundering rain.

"Stop!"

"Wait!"

"Halt!"

The voices of his pursuers roared in his wake, making his heart shrivel with their other-realm taint as tit pierced his ears. He could feel the weight of magic in the words but his heart and mind was on a rampage to find his way home. To survives as the slick strand of compulsion slipped from him with a neck cracking shake of his head.

Dashing across a three-lane road, cars violently jerked to a halt, their back tires swinging out into skids. Jhonathan persisted, pushing his body past its limits. Angry drivers slammed their hands on their steering wheels, honking horns, whilst others shook fists from their now open windows, content to brave the downpour through the mist of anger. He ran on legs pumping the weakened muscles they had remaining, arms doing their best to propel him forward as heat drilled into his ribs, his breath wheezing like a heavy smoker as the park from his childhood memories finally came into view.

There has to be something iron in there, anything to keep them away and give me a chance to get home, he thought. He knew he had to put some distance between him and his hunters. He could practically feel their breath upon his neck, his fine hairs already stood on alert. He had no idea how many tracked him, or what type of fairy's they were.

For all he knew it was the Queen herself, accompanied by a score of personal, masochistic guards. He had no time to ponder, instead he vaulted over the low fence into the park thinking of the wild curly hair of the other creature now wearing a human disguise, as he passed bleeding red painted swings. The painter watched him curiously as he weaved quickly through the mass of playground equipment, praying they contained a fragment of iron- even if only in the aged paint rusting from the rundown shed of the park monitor.

Jhonathan could sense the fairy's caution at approaching so much metal for their disguised bodies would unmask if they tried to come too close. Not to mention that myths told of iron to be poisonous to them and he had never seen the slightest fleck of it whilst in the Queen's palace; so, his faith in the legends was more than absolute. The fairy's would have to take the long way and trail the path edging the park, and by that time he would have disappeared from their wretched, hateful sight.

But what of the two who had helped me escape?, he questioned himself. He was unsure of them, especially the amber afro haired fairy. Besides, they were now cloaked in glamour. Why would they hide like that if they meant him no harm, and after he had given Akantha the badge prized by those who had freed him from the chains of the Queen? Did the fairy now cloaked in dark human skin, trestles of silver-grey hair hanging from a heart shaped face set with too big eyes deserve the honour? He was unsure, even though she had saved him from rotting inside the belly of a dragon. Jhonathan stopped to take a breath, his head held low to his knees while he gasped in great heaves of air. His mind still a whirl with questions and thoughts that his brain was unable to process because of the speed they were pirouetting around in his head. Taking one last deep gulp of air, the rain soaking his grimy body cleansing it of horrors, he checked over his shoulders in spasms of anxious terror. He began to run again, questioning his own sanity at the mass of confusion flooding his mind. The badge he had gifted the fairy was precious to the P.E.T Empathisers who had died, charred to ash by the Queen's battle dragon, to save his life.

    It was true that he had started to believe their species was capable of small kindnesses. Especially after the wild burnt orange haired one had healed his mortal body, not once but twice; but she had turned out to be the same as all the others, desperate to claim him as her PET- just like the Queen had. Jhonathan shivered, internally vowing; *I'll never go back there again, never belong to someone other than myself, never.*

I would rather die.

Chapter 2

Shayleigh

Shayleigh didn't understand why her human; Jhonathan had run away from her. Her heart bled at the wound of betrayal it sliced through her. Why had he acted so abruptly, so out of character for such a sweet PET? Maybe she was too rash with her affections and frightened him away; after all he was only human and both her and Akantha had limited knowledge of their understanding. She flicked her tail in agitation. Maybe her attempts at man's kindness had infringed on some ritual unknown to her. Or was it that he found her too ugly and beastly to allow her to look after him?

A heavy hand settled on her shoulder, and she felt the comforting pierce of fairy talons beneath her friend's mortal glamour. She turned watery eyes to Akantha, her sideways lids blinking rapidly to stop the torrent of tears. "Never have I ever had a PET not like me." She sniffled "I know I am unattractive, but that's never had an effect on anyone's PETs before. Akantha, what did I do wrong; why doesn't he like me?"

"Come on Shay, you know you're not ugly-" Shay gave her a gleaming glare encrusted in a subtle threat of magic. Akantha sighed, pulling her into a friendly embrace, the clenching in her heart eased with the comfort and her thrashing tail calmed its irrational whipping of the tarmac. "Shay, you're the kindest fairy I know and for our species that truly is a rarity. You just have to remember that these humans are not- they are not like the minor fairy's of the wild wood that flit and dance around you in praise of your attentions. They have complex minds Shay- you can't simply warm their hearts towards fairy's after what our race has historically put them through; no matter that we are not ancestors or the Queen."

"Oh Akantha, no wonder he ran. He thought I would chain him as she did; take his freedom - own his soul. I never meant-"

Akantha squeezed her shoulder, "I know."

"I only wanted-"

"It's okay Shay."

"But I-"

"Look," Akantha released her, stepped back and bore her eyes into her friend's. "Humans might not be minor faeries but they're still not as smart as us so stop the pity ball and let's hunt ourselves a mortal before he gets himself, or us, into any more trouble." She sighed, shoving her friend forwards, the torrent of hammering raindrops slid down her skin as if she were a greater mer-creature.

"You know- for all the magic I possess," Shayleigh's mind wandered, "I still haven't mastered the craft of the weather." She sighed as they made their way down the claustrophobic alley, her heavy water-logged tail sweeping behind her as they left the portal pierced with the dragon's tooth and hidden by a veil of magic, behind.

Akantha led the way, pausing for moments to sniff in the fresh, scent concealing rain. But downpour or not, her fairy senses were more than strong enough to follow the tint of a being recently passed through a magical portal.

"For a human, he runs fast." Shayleigh chuckled, excited by the hunt that bubbled her predatory instinct alive, again within her very soul. Her heart finally calming from her upset and instead setting its beat to elation at the long, overdue gaieties of the hunt.

The Queen had forbidden her such privilege, confining her to the kitchens where she slaved about her regular day's routines.

She did not mind. Or at least she thought she didn't. Since falling into the human realm her opinions had become muddled, her comprehension of life had shifted, like the unveiling of a mask to discover someone unknown, in a place you always assumed to be there.

Pushing her ponderous thoughts aside, Shayleigh ran, barely remembering to keep her mortal looking feet on the ground as her skin flaps caught air and her tail began to steer her glide. If Jhonathan had seen her, he would have laughed at her childish charade of a plane, with her glamoured- human arms stretched out. Akantha just inches behind her, imitating her stance all apart from her chin which she stuck out.

Together the fairy's appeared like the legends of vampires, cosmetically beautiful; a tornado of rusted amber curls and shimmering grey hair whipping behind them with their effortless speed.

They tailed him as he ran through the alleys slamming past humans, breathing almost upon his neck, until he recklessly darted across the street, giving them pause to wonder at the vehicles only recorded in myths and legends among their species.

"Remind me why we don't just use compulsion on him?" Shayleigh asked, head tilted as she watched him run, concern etching her brow at the crimson trail he left in his wake. She licked her lips. It must have hurt. Her poor little– human. Why the silly thing kept running from her was-

"Are we going across?" Akantha questioned, a hand waving before Shayleigh's glazed face. "If we don't go soon those mechanical contraptions will start up again, and I for one do not like the way they reek of metal."

Shayleigh shook her head, grabbing at her friend's arm and pulling her aside. They locked eyes. "I don't want him harmed Akantha. I feel like- I- like I-" She sighed, running a hand through her hair, her head tilted as she furrowed her brow.

"It's like I'm on the cusp of some wondrous discovery within a padlocked minefield of memories but the darn thing keeps slipping just out of reach."

Akantha mirrored Shayleigh's frown. "Are you alright? I'm worried about you. This realm is making you—I don't know- unwell?"

"Unwell?" she considered, tilting her head and blinking her sideways eyelids.

"Well, since we arrived you seemed caught up in memories and shadowed from reality. Shay, is there something I should know? If you're sick I can help you. I admit I cannot heal like you, but there is magic in herbs too."

"I'm fine-let's go. I can't- discuss this right now; later- okay." She smiled at her friend, straightened her arms to mimic the shell-shocked pedestrians as they watched the scene Jhonathan had left in his wake and once again chased after him.

Chapter 3

Akantha

Akantha worried about the state of Shayleigh's mental health. With all the things she had experienced, even in the time they had become friends, Akantha wouldn't blame her if she lost it and brewed up a cursed dragon. But the shame of questioning her best friend, even if it was for her own health, weighed heavily on Akantha, like the deceit before a betrayal.

But still, she couldn't stop the thoughts that screamed at her that something was wrong with

Shayleigh. Or more importantly, one of her horrific memories had surfaced and was rattling at its jail bars? Akantha knew Shayleigh's history to be worrisome, but some of her past had been hidden even from Shayleigh herself. She had sensed it the first time they had met; it had been the night her father swore her services to the Queen. What she had done so wrong to offend her father she didn't know, nor would she likely get the chance to find out. But she had enlisted into the Queen's service under duress of disinterment and had to drown her sorrows on human ale, the only known alcohol to inhibit a fairy, to go through with his order. She was a warrior. She would endure until her father relinquished the command, but she had to believe he had an ulterior motive. For he despised the Queen and would surely not trade his only daughter for the security of his position under the new ruler.

Shayleigh had been in the kitchens that night, she had just received a beating when Akantha walked in. The beating was sentenced because of an alleged accusation that the Queen didn't like her dessert that day. It was a load of dragon dung, then and now. But no one dared argue with her. Even upon entering the palace Akantha had heard of the Queen's dislike for the fairy named Shayleigh; who she had working as the runt, scrubbing and swabbing every available surface in the kitchens.

Some fairy's said it was Shayleigh's punishment for the past. Whilst others said she was too hideous and stupid for anything but menial tasks, and she should think herself lucky the Queen had kept her on in service, instead of abandoning her to whatever fate allowed her in the wildwoods with the Halflings who escaped her culling.

Both fairy's had needed a drink that day and Akantha had spent what felt like an age rattling on to her new, bruised friend as voices whispered tales of how ugly and unworthy of her time Shayleigh was. It was strange, she thought now, the voices that had confided in her that night, through the intoxication of her mind, had vanished with the sunrise. She had not heard them since. Come to think of it, she had not considered Shayleigh ugly thereafter. Only different, unique.

She knew deep down that she should interrogate her, until the bars of that jailed memory shook loose, so she could finally help her deal with the darkness that ate away at her without her knowledge. It was just fairy's luck that Shay couldn't heal herself.

Following the redhead across the road, stance ready for attack, Akantha weaved between the mechanical contraptions stinking of metal and sulphur. She eyed the humans who dared to glance her way, her fangs flicking through the glamour flashing their deadly warning in what appeared to them as a mirage.

She was ready for whatever fleshy creature passed them as she followed Shayleigh, eyes scanning, arms held tensely at her sides. She would be a fearsome sight for any human to behold if her glamoured skin didn't veil her true form. She was a mountain fairy and a warrior; she was prepared for anything–anything except the pungent stench that burnt the tiny hairs in her nose.

"Iron." She breathed, turning to assess the fenced metal maze of torturous looking contraptions.

"W-what is it?" Shayleigh sighed next to her, her bottom lip pouting, a slight breach of her fang piercing her human glamour. "He taunts us Akantha. Do you think this is play to him? I have never seen a mortal game, not even the young ones the Queen has tending her gardens, though I suppose if they did, she would have them see the era of their ways with a punishment befitting a fairy criminal."

Akantha often wondered why her father had enlisted her into the service of the dreaded Queen. It's not like there was ever any need for her to visit the mainland from her frozen island in the south-west. Her father had never explained. The dynamic leader of the mountainous land had merely bent under the oppressive ruling of the Queen. Years ago,, she had taken the throne by force and decreed all those who rose against her were to be executed in the most painful of ways–death by iron. But her, her father, nor even their people had stood in her bloody path to the throne. Being smart enough to know they were too few to stop her troops advances, they cowardly stood aside. Watching as the new power slaughtered her way through family and foe, dispelling any of those with even the faintest hint of royal blood from their realm and the world alike.

Shaking the conundrum from her mind she answered Shayleigh, who still stood, head tilted, tail whipping back and forth, awaiting her verdict, "No, I think he is genuinely afraid. I think he means to protect himself in this maze of iron. You must remember Shay; these humans are created irrational. For one moment they like you and the next, have savagely bitten off your thumb."

Harrumphing, Shayleigh agreed. "But why then did he gift you that disk? It must have been precious to him for him to have kept it for so long. I would have merely thrown the dusty thing away."

"This-this thing?" She pulled the pin from her uniform breaches pocket and rolled it smoothly over her long human nails, allowing the object to taint her glamour from flesh tones to slate flecked with dust and silver. "I don't know, maybe he simply wished to be rid of it." She flicked it into the air, snatching it amid the daggers of rain that savagely hit the pin, a stream of ashy tears bleeding from the words embedded on its face. Akantha swept an eager thumb over the mess revealing;

P.E.T

Chapter 4

Shayleigh

Shayleigh stroked her chin horn. Worn smooth with time, the appendage was most calming to her muddled thoughts. The human realm around her would only see a young girl with a birth defect, so great was her glamour. It hid her from fang to sleek long tail.

She was the perfect imitation of a human child, for most fae glamours allowed their casters a youthful appearance. The only part of her slightly obscured was the rather bulbous chin that concealed her spiralled chin horn. What a sight she must have been, she thought, chuckling internally as she imagined herself uglier than even before. If the male fairy's thought her form sickening before, they should see her as a human; damn if she wasn't the ugliest creature alive.

No doubt uglier than my fairy self, she contemplated, her mind slipping off track once again before musing on the puzzle that was human. She wondered if she was more or less repulsive to Jhonathan in her glamoured form. If he would be less afraid of her, she might adopt it more often. She hated the fear she felt in others judgemental eyes. They had no idea of the trials she had been through, for fae sake she couldn't even remember half of them.

She turned her souring thoughts to Jhonathan instead. "You would think such an endearment as Pet would not offend Jhonathan." She shook her head, her afro curls bouncing around her deformed face. "It is merely a word of endearment and yet he appears terrified as if I could turn on him and beat him senseless. As if I would ever harm him."

"Perhaps." Akantha mussed, "although maybe its meaning in the human tongue is foreign to us. And no one, no one would ever believe you capable of harming a PET."

Akantha rubbed the pad of her thumb back and forth over the badge. "I wonder what use it is to humans. Jhonathan mentioned retrieving it from the ashes of those who helped him escape the Queen's chains, but he didn't say anything about them being fairy, and by the swell of magic pulsing from this thing I would say they were most definitely of fairy origin. Could it mean that someone is fighting back against the evil Queen and her steel hold on our realm?" She studied the object, its deeply grooved letters formed by intricate chains. The piece was beautiful, but for some reason it felt sad even though she could feel the taint of a fairy's magic heavily protecting it.

Obviously, it is not meant to harm our kind, for if it was it would be cast of iron or at least carry a trace of its atoms, but I sense none. In fact,, I sense no ill will within this creation, only a resonating sadness. So, what purpose does it hold? What secrets?"

Shayleigh studied the object, a stream of sweat dripping down her spine despite the cold consistent downpour. She reached out her hand to trace the indented words. "It seems to me they are what humans call obviations." Her eyes sparkled, a thick sheen broke out on her forehead and her head straightened in a sudden snap of attention. "A common signifier of the current time period I think."

Akantha stared at her, eyes wide, "Shay, how do you know-"

She rammed a palm into her head, her sideways lids squinting as she emitted a low growl. "I don't- I -"

"DROP THE WEAPON FAE SCUM!"

A fist, undoubtedly iron, with a polearm of ash to strengthen its retribution smashed a blood-curdling scream from Shayleigh, upon impact her skin sizzled and popped as if she were pig roasting over a spit. She fell to her knees in agony, her eyes blanching, falling and turning grey, a single spark shining in their depths like a shooting star before its final voyage.

A deep, sickening hollowness seared into Shayleigh's abdomen, tunnelling on and on, burying itself in her blood steam and expanding to her organs. Her body crumpled; her muscles weak with the poison. Her eyes fluttered shut as the empty nothingness only iron could inflict, imprisoned Shayleigh within her mind. As the sickness grew with the prolonged touch of its white-hot surface to her skin, her tail twitched spasmodically until finally, blessedly; all went black.

**

Akantha

Akantha caught her, instantly shedding her glamour and snapping her wings out in a striking path of gore into the chest of their attacker, his leather shirt peeling like the skin from a banana. Stumbling back in an agonised cry their beefy assailant was replaced by another. The female retrieved the fallen polearm as their third attacker knelt over their fallen comrade, one hand pressed to his shoulder his eyes flashed black.

An instant later the polearm thrust at her. She dodged. Whipped her wing out to knock it off balance from its current path to Shayleigh's unconscious form and hissed at the searing burning through her wing tip. She slashed right. Her long talons shredded dirt. The human jabbed left, iron hissing by her bat ear, her sonar shaking unsteadily with its closeness. Then a blinding flash of light. Her attention flicked to the fallen man who vanished in the apparition.

Temporarily blinded by the shock of light Akantha didn't notice the crafty skid of the polearm along the surface of the ground. Until it hit her foot, crumpling her to the ground before her assailant struck again, smashing into her chest, the impact of the iron leaving her gasping for breath. She blinked twice before comprehension dawned. She lay crumpled around the iron fist leaching the strength from her body. *There was no way an ordinary human could have caught her in the millisecond it took to glance away*, she thought as she stared at a wicked smile with the slightest hint of fangs. The deep holo spidering of iron had her beautiful grey skin turning a sickly yellow as the poison finally, blessedly, tugged her into unconsciousness.

Chapter 5

Jhonathan

Jhonathan's feet slammed into the squelching mud of the soggy park, splashing dots around his legs. He swept his shaggy fringe of midnight hair from his eyes, slicking it back with the heavy rain water.

Hitting the edge of the park, Jhonathan vaulted over the fence encompassing the children's play area in a veil of assumed safety. No longer did he feel the proverbial scythe scratch at his neck, as he- the fairy's prey, outwitted the treacherous creatures. Did they really think he had learnt nothing of their weaknesses whilst enslaved in the fairy realm?

The pretentious species never looked beneath their position to notice the going on's of the PETs. Jhonathan had always listened with rapt attention, desperate to find a way home, a way to freedom or the power to fight them. One day such information tweaked his ears as a group of guards returned from their duty patrolling the portals to the human realm, keeping what they called vermin–out. But one particular guard; new he gathered, intercepted a perpetrator. He came back squealing in agony, his veins bulging and contracted, an insipid yellow leaching the natural colour. Consuming it as it pulsated, like a web of disease, it splintered from the impaling tip of an arrow head.

That's when the door to the PET cells were opened and a young woman was unchained from the leash at her throat and ordered to remove the arrow head from the fairy's body. No one had understood what was happening. That they were giving the PETs access to their greatest vulnerability; iron.

Free and armed with the arrowhead the woman took her chances, warning the fairy back until, he had later been told, she had escaped from the Queen's castle. But rumour had, she angered the Queen so much, she set lose her blood trackers to retrieve her. The woman had never stood a chance. The next time he saw her she was no more than a human husk enchanted by their will.

The only way out was with the help of the P.E.T Empathisers, as Jhonathan had discovered- but even they weren't invincible. Trusting the two fairy creatures had been his only choice after the Empathisers had disappeared. Finding their ashen remains still disturbed his waking thoughts, but then as now, he had no time to dwell on it- for home was finally coming into view, and he no longer sensed the females hunting him.

The lane he crossed was empty, the heavy flow of rain making it look like more of a river plagued by oil, as an old man paused to frown at his shredded clothes from beneath the comfort of a shielding umbrella.

The tarmac bit searing grazes into the souls of his filthy bare feet as he sloshed through the collecting drifts of flood water. The pain emanating from his throbbing feet barely registered before he blocked it out, locking all feeling away as he had come to learn how to do by the persistent wicked hand of the Queen.

Red bricked, terris houses lined the street as he sped past the old man still transfixed on him, an explosion of shock and bewilderment staining his wrinkled face. Jhonathan turned into the cul-de-sac and slowed to a jog, his chest heaving with each wheezing breath that escaped his lungs. Within a few seconds he managed to force his hammering heart back into its natural rhythm, just moments before reaching his home; his salvation.

His feet automatically stepped forwards, tracing the route he had trod for years before his faemonic abduction. He barely even heard the call of shelter from a mother wren to her fledgeling, barely heard the slap of his feet on the tarmac, barely heard it change to a crunch of shifting gravel, as he made his way up the small drive.

He hobbled past a rusty red mini parked in the driveway, rosary beads hanging from its rear-view mirror. It seemed nothing had changed and yet in his mind he was reeling, stunned into numbness due to his surroundings. His body no longer felt the pound of rain on his skin, just the deft beat of his heart as he fought to tame its wildness. Suddenly his hand lifted of its own accord to strike the white front door with a rattling conviction.

For the longest three seconds of his existence Jhonathan's heart retreated into submission, his bruised rib cage finally getting a chance to recover as the organ swelled in anticipation. He stumbled to his knees on the porch step, knocking over a plant pot, but never hearing the sharp crack of the pottery, as his senses focused in on the door. A slow tred of footsteps gradually increased in volume. Then silence, before the soft click of a lock sounded. The long slide of a safety latch, and the clank of its chain as it fell free, had his Adam's apple dancing up and down his Sahara trachea.

The rush of blood in his ears couldn't block out the voice that preceded the click as the handle turned in agonising slowness. His traitorous heart played a staccato as a mellow voice sang out a soft, questioning 'hello', and the door opened an inch. A cascade of long dark hair was all he could peek at with the slow agony of his mother's reveal, as she eased the front door open.

Smash!

His mother spun from the door, shrieking her terror, she ran towards whatever had happened, leaving it loose enough for Jhonathan to push open and catch a glimpse of her retreating form wobbling away with the aid of a stick.

A man with thick black locks popped his head around the living room door. "It's alright mum don't rush, we don't want you to have another fall." The man held out a small rock, shaking his head, his eyes glancing toward Jhonathan with a deep frown furrowing his brows, as his stubborn jawline clenched. The man's face looked pale, ashen even, from the fleeting glance he got before his attention turned back to the rock in his hand. "Bloody kids threw it at the window then ran off! Rebecca's sweeping the mess up now. I think it would be best if you moved in with us for a while. Or at least until we can get things fixed."

Jhonathan strained hard to hear the voice of his brother from beneath the man's skin, his attention so focused on their conversation that he didn't acknowledge the crunch of gravel behind him. Nor did he recognise the dull, heavy thwack that would render him unconscious. His mother's words bled into his ears; "Jhonathan will return. The police are wrong. They always were. He is not dead-"

He longed to call out to her, to scream out he was there, alive and home at last. But the words clogged in his mind, his throat ceasing as he tried to work them free. But all he could do was listen and weep internally as a roughened hand dragged his body further and further from his mother's voice; until he finally lay unconscious.

Chapter 6

Akantha

Akantha flicked her attention to Shayleigh, who lay collapsed on the dirt, her tail twitching as she fought the iron's touch. Flicking her eyes around in brief assessment, Akantha sought any danger her friend might need protecting from. But there was no more danger than their impending imprisonment since they had been marched inside their cells at the point of a polearm tipped with iron. Akantha rested back on her wings, rocking slightly in their arch as she calmed her mind in an attempt to think clearly.

Something was unnerving her about their whole abduction. It had been so organised, so prepared, almost as if their attackers had lain in wait for them. But how was that possible? How had they known two fairy's would be chasing a human at that time and for that matter, why was Jhonathan not imprisoned with them? Where in Faes' name was he? Had he, a mere human, organised their faenapping?

She turned to look at Shayleigh. She had passed out as soon as they reached the vermin ridden cell, but Akantha had not. Her people possessed a stronger resilience against the poison of iron than most, that's why they were often employed as the Queen's guards. If, of course, they made it through the Queen's extensive training. However, most chose to steer clear from the vicious Queen, even though the positions she offered them were revered by the whole realm. Akantha had never wanted anything to do with her royal Evilness, but unfortunately, thanks to her not so beloved father she had no choice. She had lost respect for the old fairy the day he abandoned her into the Queen's service. She remembered his parting.

It was dawn and the Queen's scouts had come to escort her to the palace. They had been traveling for weeks just to get to the snowy mountain island south west of the Queen's palace, where her species of fairy resided. Her father had welcomed them that day like a long lost family, presenting their people from the lowliest fairy to the Barons who held positions only accountable to him; and the Queen of course. He had arranged a banquet of fine mountain delicacies served by the most loyal of PET's. But the scouts dared not stay a second longer than necessary, explaining that the Queen would have their feet if they were inept at walking the speed to her liking.

So, they had left right away, sparing only the time it took her to retrieve her belongings- minimal at best, and escorted her from the hall of her father's home. She had thought at first, he would deny her a parting farewell, for his anger at her was more obvious by the second. Yet he placed a glancing peck on her cheek, giving her the only indication that her father still loved her.

She shook the memory from her mind, thinking instead how lucky they really were, for she had been chosen that day due to her heritage. It was true that all fae would heal from the touch of iron in time, but her species; the Faemontis, could heal at almost the same speed as the instrument of iron left their skin.

Akantha lay in wait of an opportunity to strike, but none seemed to present itself, so she marked the passing of time with the ominous;

Clang,

Clang,

Clang.

Of a weapon on the cell door, which rattled with the impact. She supposed it was a strategy to strike fear into their hearts, but she was a warrior of the mountains, not some weak whelp of the fae realm, shaking in fear. *Humans are weak*, she thought, *if that's all that is required to have them submitting to fear.* The door vibrated once more before the footsteps of a hefty male receded and Shayleigh, and herself, were once again left alone.

Counting in a slow, steady verse to ten Akantha funnelled her magic like her father had taught her when she was young. She let the starburst of colours form in her soul, moulding them into bolts as her eyes began to glow. Her body vibrated like a purring cat from every cell her power broke forth, and she channelled it with the vicious strike of one unveiled wing into the old-fashioned lock.

Sparks of blue-tipped bolts danced around the inside of the key hole, crackling and hissing angrily as the iron veins annulled its magic, quashing it into a harmless light that bounced freely back into the cell until its magic spluttered out. Akantha roared her frustration, her talons and fangs lengthening, a sheen of sweat broke out across her forehead. Her wing tip shook with the exertion she expelled in a magical assault landing her firmly, but painfully, on her butt.

All attempts to escape failed. On previous attempts, Akantha always counted to ten after she heard the heavy footsteps leave.

She had attacked every point of perceived weakness within the cell she could exploit, but to no avail, apart from weakening her state of magic.

Shayleigh stirred again, this time rubbing at her chin horn with a look of pain etching her face, before she jolted awake from her splayed pillow of rusty, wild hair. Eyes wide and sparkling green, Shayleigh turned to her, swallowed, then licked her lips to speak in the softest of whispers, each word escaping her mouth warbled as her body shook. "Akantha are we- are we home?'

With barely a tilt of her lips Akantha huffed out a "no." The single most important word she could say to Shayleigh before Akantha felt her body shift, its energy drained, magic depleted, her body slumped to the rocky floor, her head thudding harshly before Shayleigh's numb legs could catch her.

Chapter 7

Shayleigh

Throat dryer than the sands of Seelie beach. Shayleigh swallowed, her throat anchoring itself like a fly in a web. "Akantha wake up." She rasped, giving the fairy's a little shake, only to have her eyes roll following a quick flitter of her eyelids. She was exhausted, Shayleigh deduced after examining the confines of their prison and noticing no more marks on her friend's ashy skin than the one the humans first put there. "It'll be okay." She whispered, "Don't worry Shay, I'm a warrior, a fighter. I will recover and then- then we will make our escape." She stretched around her friend, positioning her so she could rest her heavy bat eared head on her lap. Her other hand stroked rhythmically at her chin horn as her tail swept a crescent in the dusty stone floor, lurching as it hit on a vein of iron she thought.

She harboured only the vaguest recollection of the journey to the cell due to the consistent prods of iron and the hypnagogic hallucinations it was disposing her to. She barely stayed in a lusive state to view Acantha's numerous attempts to break down the cell door to, undoubtedly, attain their freedom. But what she did remember clearly, or at least she thought she did, was the soulless black eyes of an ancient staring out of the husk of a boy. It was mere minutes before she was blinded from staring at his horrifying eyes, minutes as Shayleigh was snatched from beside her by a stout round woman who disappeared in the blink of an eye before returning first for a human and then for her.

The woman's powers were inhuman, as she touched Akantha's tacky skin she could feel the recognition of something faemonic inside of her. She was no human and no ancient resided in her. She was a Halfling. A filthy outlawed abomination and no wonder they were so disregarded, she was busy helping the human's fairy's nab her. A few times, during the skin itching teleportation, she lost consciousness.

But still, she remembered being escorted down a tunnel of corridors, delirious with the iron sickness poisoning her. Back in the fae realm if those beneath the Queen's rule dared not to congratulate her on her hunt they would be executed on the spot by the power of her magic.

The male clad in midnight leather, his voice gruff and soulless, ordered them to move. He jabbed at them constantly, annulling their magic and weakening their fairy abilities, along with their human glamours that shifted form consistently, weakening their powers and dulling their strength.

If they hadn't had the iron at their backs as they marched along, Akantha would have undoubtedly taken them all. She was so strong, much stronger than an ordinary fairy when facing the poisons of iron. But it had weakened her magic too much for her to retaliate, or even speed away.

But of all the strange revelations Shayleigh had ever had, a new found freedom came upon her with the first strike of iron on her skin. A feeling of chains being lifted every time the poison touched her body.

Maybe she consoled herself, it was an out of skin experience, one close to dying. But something inside her had changed. Her thoughts seemed clearer, her vision sharper. Suddenly Akantha murmured in Shayleigh's lap, drawing her attention from her musings as she held her ear closer to hear.

"Help me."

Her voice was so soft, so weak; Shayleigh had never heard it's like, not since she was under the Queen's condemning eyes. "All will be well my friend." She soothed, stroking at the fairy's long silver hair instead of calming herself with the comfort of rubbing her chin horn.

Skin throbbing with the presence of iron she could feel veined throughout the cell, she pulled her strength together searching out her cowering magic in the back of her soul and coaxed it forwards to run wildly through her veins. Stroking and petting it with her mind, encouraging it to be brave in the presence of all the iron that surrounded them. Strong enough to heal their friend. Her companion, who was her only hope of escaping such a prison, thanks to her mountain fairy heritage.

With Akantha cradled in her lap, she willed her magic from the core of her soul, moulding and shaping it with taloned hands. Smoothing and rounding it's pulsing green edges that matched her aventurine eyes, inlaid with a rich yellowy-gold. Shayleigh tilted her friend's mouth open and pressed the glowing orb inside.

Unaccustomed to the taste of such raw, untapped magic, Shayleigh watched as Akantha greedily swallowed the glowing orb, her soul accepting its nourishment to replenish her exhausted and bruised body.

Just as Akantha bolted upright, Shayleigh slumped to the floor, a wicked smile on her face, her eyes now a dull, but determined green and a twitch of her tail as it wrapped around one of Akantha's slender wrists. "Your magic is less affected than mine. Free us-" Her breath became raspy, her silky tail released her wrist and slumped to the floor as she watched Akantha from slitted eyes, she knelt next to her with a quizzical brow.

"Shay your magic tastes different; stronger, like the life force of an evergreen Prosithian tree; the tree of life and ultimate healing, the tree of the Queen. She turned to Shayleigh, seeing her through the eyes of such power was like seeing a trapped grown fairy chained within the husk of someone else's creation; the husk of a fool.

" What did you d-"

Suddenly a booming voice echoed throughout the room, a thick sense of hatred palpable on the air around them that seeped through the little key hole.

"What the hell is going on in there?"

Chapter 8

Jhonathan

Jhonathan woke with a deep pounding headache threatening to shatter his skull from the inside Groaning he blinked dry heavy eyelids, to reveal blurred shining lights and shadows swaying a dizzying rhythm above him. He grasped at his head, trying to rub the pain away. He remembered his mother used to say that it was holistically possible to induce a small state of recovery with the aid of rubbing and tending a wound. But instead of the skin of his forehead he found a waded pad of what felt like towelled ice plastered there.

"Don't touch that." A trill voice demanded, knocking his hand from the ice. "I've got to get the swelling down." She huffed.

Swelling? Well, that would explain the throbbing in his head. But how the hell had that happened, and who was she?

Licking his dry lips, he cautiously approached his predicament "Am I in a hospital?"

"No." Came the firm, almost indignant reply.

"Are you one of Her Guards?" He whispered suspiciously, his Adam's apple quivering with each word he formed.

"No." She patted his shoulder, her small hands warm if not a little abrasive. "Now calm down and rest."

Jhonathan sighed. For once he actually wished for the fairy's. Not the Queen's Guards to drag him back into slavery as her PET, but the fairy's who had helped him escape; they would have healed his head. The one with the rusty amber afro hair had that power, a rare power from what he knew of their kind. The only other being that he'd heard whisperings of baring that power was the Queen. But she was also the one who wanted to keep him- as her Pet. God, life couldn't get more complicated than it was now. He didn't even know where he was. One moment he was free of the fairy realm, running from the fairy's and guards. The next, he was kneeling on the front porch of his home, the door open. His brothers' eyes had glanced at him, before moving swiftly on like he was nothing and then the emptiness of unconsciousness struck Jhonathan in the side of the head. Upon waking, he harboured the idea that someone had overpowered him with the effect of an instrument cracked against his head, laying him out cold, by the evidence of his throbbing skull.

The left side of his temple throbbed as if in confirmation. But why? What had he done to them and who the hell else wanted a piece of him?

He blinked rapidly again, watching as the colours slowly morphed into focus. The ceiling above him was curiously painted a pale blue, patches of white he assumed to be clouds were staggered over its base. A sudden flare of colour caught his attention, and he jerked his head with blinding pain to follow its course. It was the tiny flitting wings of an emperor butterfly as it fluttered down on an invisible breeze to land on the shoulder of the girl nursing him, before slipping into a spiracle behind her slender pointed ear.

Jhonathan's face fell as he watched the butterfly (fairy mirage his mind corrected), disappeared into the midnight skinned girl who tended his creaking head.

The tiny tilt of its wings, joy at finally reaching home, was locked down. The stern pursing of his lips taking place. His heart thumping hard enough to bruise his ribs with its demand to be lightened with the happiness of joy once more, Jhonathan let his eyes rest heavily on the girl before asking "Why am I here?'

Bright amber globes captured his, their pupils narrowing as a smear rippled over her plump lips.

"Yo Dude, ignore Sharlami she's half — and they're always touchy," chuckled a lanky teenager in grey sweats and a Nike tee. His smile seemed genuine, his front teeth breaking the gap between his parted lips as he walked up to Jhonathan, holding out a hand, his caramel skin giving away no hint of fairy heritage.

"Come on, take it." The teen waggled it before his own. Jhonathan begrudgingly conceded to accept the hand and rose from the old sofa, watched over by the butterfly fairy; Sharlami.

"Come on man, don't look so beat. It's cool here, we're all cool here, I mean Con can be a real pain in the ass, but otherwise you're safe. We all are." He held his hands wide and turned to encompass the room, knocking into the coffee table in his haste.

"Damn it Tim, look where you're bloody going." Snarled a young man using a piece of his tattered checkered shirt's tail to mop up a sticky black that bubbled like tar from a bright red can.

Jhonathan jumped, not having noticed anyone else in the room.

"Oh, that's Kevin," Tim waved a hand at the irritated guy whose eyes now shone like stars in the night. "He pops up everywhere he's not wanted." Kevin flipped him the bird and Tim chuckled.

Jhonathan was getting the sense that maybe his situation wasn't as dire as he first perceived if Tim could tease a fairy and walk away with his life and limbs intact.

"Come on, this way. God; you look like you could do with fattenin' up." Tim placed a guiding hand on Jhonathan's shoulder, steering him through corridors of peeling wallpaper and scuff scratched tiles. A turn to the left and Tim finally stopped the barrage of information, spewing from his mouth like a confetti cannon; he was so elated. The persistent pressure on the back of his shoulder ebbed as his head throbbed hard enough to squeeze tears from his eyes and Tim pushed him down onto a stool.

"What the hell possessed you to bring him in here, in that state? "

The half-garbled noise of Tim's reply wobbled around his overstuffed mouth, the smell of rich tomato and mature cheese had his stomach raging like a chained beast.

A loud laugh rumbled, followed by the tearing of something, but Jhonathan couldn't see what was happening before his blinding eyes. He could barely hear a thing above the incessant pitch of ringing in his ears as the pounding in his head became his only focus.

"Why the hell did you get him up? Can't you see he's still reeling from the blow of that bloody club you hit him with? Gods Tim sometimes you're so stupid."

"But–Axel–he-"

Chapter 9

Akantha

Shayleigh had given Akantha her magic to wield in order to escape the confines of the iron veined cell they were imprisoned in. Never before had Shayleigh shared her magic with her and now she knew why, for the full extent of it was coursing through her veins, crackling and snapping at her to free it in a torrent of power. Oh, how she envied Shayleigh for the power she never imagined her having. It sizzled and popped in tiny demands throughout her soul, ready to explode and rain retribution on them all. It was a greedy angry swirl of aventurine fury. Inside her own magic answered its call to arms, spiralling and pooling into a crater amassed to hoard its strength and funnel it around Akantha's body as swiftly as possible, whipping her own magic of lightning blue fire into a rage with it, demanding they strike, strike out with all the power they possessed.

Magic begging for release Akantha set her hands at eye level as she sighted the keyhole, taking deep calming breaths so as not to disrupt the power's course when she struck, for the lock was indeed one of the smallest targets she had ever had to destroy.

Relaxed, but quietly confident, her ministrations to her core of magic would be imminent, Akantha shifted to kneel firmly on one knee, her large wing spanned tallows flared out so the tip of her fingers could practically spear the keyhole.

The cold bite of iron veining the cell nipped and bit at her like vampiric fairy's in the night. It seeped her energy leaving her lethargic as she fought to coil the magic deep within her, protecting and harbouring it for her opportune moment to escape. Her stomach tightened with her efforts as she fought the nausea it brought on.

A sudden mellow thud echoed around her, her sonar senses tuning in as more stomping resounded, giving way to the image of heavy footfalls descending steps not too far away from them. A hefty bolt slid, echoing vibrations around the strong, thick arms of their in-prisoner as a dense steel door was ripped open. The room which he was exiting was large and empty except for the stairs and cases, barrels and shelves which her sonar bounced around, giving her a basic map of the room.

Akantha listened harder, knowing her chance to strike and escape would come. And she , like a true warrior, would lay in wait, ready to pounce.

She tracked the males' movements through her senses, willing Shayleigh's and her own combined magic to concentrate in her palm, ready to expel with the force of a rocket, as soon as he-

Wait, there he was. The distant sound of foot falls breaking the harsh rasps coming from Shayleigh's sprawled form. Akantha listened harder, straining her fairy senses to the max, as she tracked the advancing footsteps of the man. No -not man she realised as he twirled his wrist in the vacant air of the passage way around him. A long, dense object grew, and he clasped it, running it along the lengths of the corridor in slow motion. The scraping sound of it shredding the wall intensifying with each footstep like the claws of a battle dragon grazing up the rocks of its home as it hunted and prepared to strike. He was a halfling; a filthy half breed. That's the only way he would be able to wield effective magic against so much iron. The filthy creature.

"A-kantha." Shayleigh moaned, her eyes wide and desperate, her tail flicking.

She raised a hand to silence her. "I got this," she whispered, careful not to lose her mark. She dared not turn to look at her friend. She kept her focus, steadied her breathing, and zeroed in on the tiny fleck of corridor lit from behind the crack.

The keyhole was now her sole purpose, her only thought as her breath clouded the cell. The iron webs weaved by some extraordinarily talented human or being all centred around that lock. The minute anyone opened it their imprisoning web would be broken, but Akantha feared they would already be prepared for any attack she planned. The iron weapons they wielded convinced her so. This truly was their only chance of escape and-

Thud…Thud…

Any minute now, any second and the guard patrolling them would-

Clank-

The ricochet of the blunt instrument hitting the cell rang out all around them, the iron itself-quivered like a web indicating the catch of its prey as Akantha stayed her body from shaking with the adrenalin flooding her.

Clank!

The instrument hit the door, its steel vibrating on impact. Then the slightest glimpse of fabric floated teasingly across the keyhole, blotting out the light as the third strike of the blunt object connected with the crack. Akantha's sucked up magic burst free in a bolt of energy, crackling it through the keyhole and blazing into the guards' weapon, in an explosion that shattered the lock.

Akantha couldn't help the malicious grin that spread across her heart shaped face, as she clenched her magic burnt hand to her chest, the skin bubbling and spitting from the force of the magic exploding through it. She didn't care, they were finally free of the oppressive iron cage and now she could help Shayleigh to stand and hobble out of this stinking dragon's hole.

Coaxing Shayleigh to wrap her tail around her waist Akantha began the stumbling walk to their escape, whispering;

"Shay, Shayleigh, I did it. We did it. We're free!"

Chapter 10

Shayleigh

The blazing explosion from the magic charge Akantha had unleashed had rung shrill in Shayleigh's ears moments before she wrapped her arms around her, guided her tail to circle her waist and dragged her to standing. "Come on Shay, shake it off; I know you're stronger than this – even with the iron."

The words whispered in her ears, the tones slowly becoming decipherable as her eyes roamed beneath her eyelids. Akantha moaned as she pulled one of Shayleigh's arms around her neck, and Shayleigh's heart was clenching for the pain she did not yet have the strength to heal. No doubt the power of their combined magic had been too strong not to leave its mark on Akantha's pale grey skin. That's why Magia Mutuat; magic lending had been forbidden.

The costs to the wielder were too great, for only the powerful could come away from it unscathed.

Akantha knew Shayleigh would help her, but for now they had no time to waste and needed all the strength they could gather for neither of them knew the place in which they were being held. Nore did they know who, or what, was holding them prisoner.

With every step she took across the iron veined cell, supported by Akantha, a vision would rock her mind into the past;

A boy lay huddled at the base of a chair in the Queen's great hall. She had seen him from afar when tending to the Lord Coimagnus's blood trackers. He had looked at her with beseeching eyes, but she had merely tilted her head in incomprehension.

A loud bang had her jolting to the present, a quizzical knot to her brow as she tried to focus on Akantha stumbling them both towards the exit which still crackled with the blue sparks of her powers.

"Come on Shay, wake up." Akantha readjusted her hold. Shayleigh slipped, her weight dragging her into the web of iron that cast her back to memories from the past.

She stood, surrounded by the bed rolls of the Queens kitchen staff. She thought they lived no better than pets. The memories flew from her mind, replaced by an incomprehensive form and a subtle tilt to her head. She was young, maybe only in her third year or so in the Queen's service. She skipped to her bed like she always did, careful to stay away from what had become the common area. Reaching her bedroll, she found three fat seya beans nestled in the hay and a small rusty nail bent to resemble some kind of ring.

"Shay- Shay!"

The call of Akantha was loud, but she could not steer away from the ring of the past as she slipped it onto her finger and screamed-

"I'm sorry, I'm sorry – hold on." Akantha yelled, pulling her from the doorway they had crashed into. "It'll be okay, I'll get you away from all this iron-"

Iron, that was what the little ring had been made of. But why had someone put it there? It was obviously for her, she had thought as she screamed, crumpling to the floor,, tail thrashing, body ceasing and mind reeling from one question. Why she was surrounded by servants and where her fam-

"Nearly there- "

Family had gone?

"Here, just a little bit further and yes, yes that's its Shay open your eyes sweet dew."

Shayleigh's eyes fluttered open to the present. Taking a deep breath, she turned a wicked smile on Akantha.

"You did it." She rasped, "But how?"

"Our combined magic-" she huffed, her lungs still struggling with all the smoke. "Iron cannot touch our magic–it weakens and destroys it, but I knew if I just caught the guard at the right time I could-" She paused to cough as they stumbled to the door, sliding through the blown open appendage.

"- I could negate the irons impact within the cell walls by exploding our magic on the other side and that guard just so happened to be stupid enough to try and intimidate us by smacking the cell, in doing so he provided the perfect platform for our explosion– brilliant!" Akantha gazed up at Shayleigh, her pupils twitching.

"Shay are you alright?"

Shayleigh tilted her head to the side, using her free hand to stroke her chin horn. Her brow creased heavily, her hair dancing around her as she sought to dispel the confusion; or was it understanding that was overwhelming her mind. "I- I think I remembered something. A boy. Seya beans and an iron ring." Akantha raised a dark eyebrow.

"Iron hallucination?"

"Maybe." She mused.

Together the friends stumbled over the creature tormenting and imprisoning them. His batten had vanished with the impact of their magic, in a shower of thick silvery rain that glittered like the childish sleight of hand a human posing as a wizard might use. Pathetic she thought, standing above him, her talon hovering over his hand.

He should be taught a lesson. A voice from her past instructed. A memory of a fairy with golden blond hair, streaked with green earthy vines was triggered in her mind. She had found a Halfling, a low serving boy, listening at the door, the door where Shayleigh stood watching the scene unfold. The boy had begged forgiveness and the cosmic blue-eyed fairy had laughed, incanting a spell to wipe the hearing from his ears unless he was being spoken directly to by a full-blooded, superior fairy.

Her eyelids blinked inwards and her punishing talon, about to snap the man's wrist, stilled along with the unconscious strike of her tail.

"Shay come on," Akantha urged. "We have to escape! What if there are more of them?"

Knowing Akantha was right, Shayleigh pressed on, leaving the man in their wake as they moved as fast as they could down corridor after corridor of locked doors. The bright fluorescent light of overhead bulbs irritated her eyes; even in her glamour.

"Where are we?"

"In some kind of store room, I think." Akantha replied, as her hand stroked the embossed letters of a large plastic drum- marked water. Shayleigh pushed her friend's helping embrace away. Instead standing on her own, shakily, but more competent to observe her surroundings. There were big holding shelves packed with metal sealed foods, large boxes of things called crisps, and drums everywhere full of liquids from water to milk. But at the far corner lay something different, a brick receded into the wall. "Akantha."

"I see it."

"Come on-"

Together the two picked their way amongst the containers to the darkened recess sealed with a boarded door. Smiling a little fang, the two wearily peered through.

Chapter 11

Akantha

Akantha's sharp eyes scanned the room beyond the wooden door, falling on metal appliances dripping a constant pat, pat of water from a spout. Another amenity glowed with red light rings, a pot of something bubbling atop. Sniffing the air, she caught the scent of many blended spices and a touch of sharpness.

Some kind of sustenance she thought as she listened to the whir of a fan extracting the steam above it. *That's good.* She mused. *A fan means we're on an outside wall which in conclusion deduces freedom isn't far away. Shay will be happy we're so close to freedom. But then again, if we are not and it was a misconception Shay would surely panic.* She really should tell her, but she didn't want to get her hopes up that the actual door to their freedom lay in this room, not when she was acting so strange. Akantha knew something was amiss. In all the time she had known her, Shay had never acted this way, nor bore so much raw power as she had in the cell. It was almost as if she was a completely different fairy.

Glamour fully back in place, with her strength slowly returning, Akantha silently slipped open the boards, hissing as her burnt palm withered in blistering agony. "Hurry." She whispered to Shayleigh. "It won't be long before the creatures return for the spoils of their boiling creation, so we have to find a way out fast."

Together they tiptoed silently at only one third of their fully strengthened fairy speed. "Let's try this one," Shayleigh said, clasping a large grey handle and tugging, the huge white door before them creaked and popped like a suction seal was breaking. Both friend's brows furrowed as quizzical faces peered around the thick rubber edged door into the chilled breeze of a walk-in fridge.

"Curious."

"Didn't you read about human lifestyles in school?" Shayleigh asked, tilting her head, her sideways eyelids blinking. Akantha turned to her with a sneer.

"Seriously? You actually listened to all that?"

Shayleigh's tail twitched, tapping on Akantha's shoulder. "You didn't?" She asked, leaving Akantha to consider her question whilst closing the cold storage door and selecting a far more worn one.

"Well, only to what could leak through my headphones, not that anyone saw them; my cousin Talya cast them invisible." She sniggered. "Besides, I thought you said you worked in the kitchens all your life."

"Did I?"

Suddenly the door swung forwards into Akantha's hand and the two fairy's were pushed backwards as someone stepped through the doorway. They took a long deep sniff, growling under their breath.

"Can they send us." Akantha let her talons unveil from her, along with her wings as she half jumped, half took off up to balance on the doors thin seam. The human hadn't moved, he stood half inside half out, an uncompromising place to be attacked. So Akantha stayed her talons, lying in wait, as his broad frame and highly tipped nose sniffed again. But this time more subtly before turning back into the corridor yelling "What the hell are you burning now Sam?"

Akantha's thrumming heart slowed. The human had gone. He hadn't scented them, and she hadn't given away their escape or position to the enemy. Still, they had to act fast for as sure as the sun would set, the human would return and most likely with reinforcements.

"He's gone." She hissed as the door swung shut. "There must be another way out–Shay come on, look for an exit; faster."

Footsteps could be heard as they speedily yanked and pulled on handles of all kinds, searching for another way out. Akantha, wings unfurled, multi-tasked several openings at once, opening and closing them at a speed almost invisible to the human eye. Her magic was recovering along with her strength and Shayleigh, too, was acting more like herself as she pulled on handles of all sizes in their desperate need to escape. She stopped once or twice to snigger at Akantha as she struggled to navigate the counters with the broad length of her wings.

It was the second time Akantha had cut her wing on an appliance before she finally decided to detract her wings, their huge span not worth the difficulty it was causing her in the unnatural confines of a human dwelling. She pulled one last handle to a large looking cupboard, calling out to Shayleigh just as the main door twitched with the faintest vibrations of movement. The two leapt into the cupboard, slamming it shut behind them as they smacked into the wooden boards at its back with a sickening crunch. Akantha hushed Shayleigh with a hand clasping her mouth as the boards at the far end gave way under them. They toppled through to the other side, landing in a pile of limbs before a row of cover cushions sofas.

"What the-" A low rumble started from one of them. "What's happening, where-"

But before she heard anymore Shayleigh was up and bounding over to the blanketed form on the closest sofa, her eyes shining more than they had since they had both been back home in the fae realm.

"Shay-No-You must not-" Akantha cried. But it was too late to stop her, she had already whizzed past, uncaring of any dangers in the room or that their crashing through the pantry wall might have been heard by the humans in the kitchen.

Sidling around the sofa Akantha could make out the form of a human male, sitting bolt upright, a mop of greasy black hair covering his eyes. For Seelie sake what the hell is going on here? Is it some kind of human magic? Akantha shrieked, bearing down on the tattered looking male. "It's like dark magic kept running into you; a déjà vu. Either that or you're more than just some human, what exactly are you Jhonathan?"

Chapter 12

Jhonathan

A loud crash had Jhonathan jolting awake. The next thing he knew the fairy, Shayleigh, was before him stroking his arm with her silky tail as she shimmered with green vein like strands. The ribbons wove together into her cupping palm. She held out the ball of aventurine fire to him. Jhonathan didn't move.

The bat fairy was busy screaming accusations at him. The people holding him here, 'for his own good', weren't far. And the rusty haired one was offering him her help again. If life wasn't so complicated one might even grow accustomed to the brooding monotony of reality. *If only-* he thought, his choices once again came down to the best chance of achieving his own freedom.

He stared at the two fairy's blankly. The fearsome bat fairy, Akantha, had terrified him, and yet she harboured a softer side, a side that saved his life; whether it was because of her friend or not. Whereas Shayleigh seemed to be only half conscious in the world around her, like a vital part of her life was missing; or forgotten. She had saved him and healed him more times than he cared for, but still, she wanted to entrap him as her own. God would this insanity ever end? When might I choose to live my own life and do with myself as I wish?

"I meant no harm to you human," Shayleigh cooed as she stroked the side of his arm. "Beautiful human." Her head tilted, teary eyes blinking sideways "I love you; you're my PE-" Lightening fast she clasped a palm to her forehead, hissing, her features scrunched up.

"Shay what's-" The bat fairy raced towards her, but Jhonathan's own hand slipped to the suffering fairy's, before he could process his own limb's reaction. He froze, his palm resting on the rust haired fairy. She gazed down at him, squeezed his hand and smiled, gently popping the magic 'cure all' orb, into his gaping mouth before touching the same hand to her friends which rested on her shoulder, concern etched in her eyes.

He was staring up at the two fairy's and their somehow strange connection when simultaneously their eyes widened, pupils swallowing the irises entirely. Both fairy's had dropped jaws, glistening fangs sparkled with blue lightning as all at once their reforming glamours exploded revealing the fairy's they were. Then they screamed.

"Well,well,well, lookie what the human dragged in." Snarled a deep baritone from behind the fairy's convulsing on the floor. Jhonathan gazed up at the broad man with the barrel of a gun clasped, smoking in his palm.

"What the hell did you do!" Jhonathan roared, leaping from beneath the blanket covering his filthy body and standing over the fallen fairy's.

"What they deserved; it's only a shame Ashur won't let me kill the filthy fae scum."

"Yo Con, not cool!" Tim stood behind the broad man, a dark glare on his face as he patted the hand of the butterfly fairy, whispering "He don't mean it, he's just pissed he don't get to kill sommat." A larger girl elbowed her way between the bodies in the slowly crowding room to snatch at the butterfly fairy's free hand, "Come on Buttercup, let's leave it to the boys, ay?" The two snuck through the assemblage, whispering, "But he's healed, how?"

Jhonathan shook his head, folding his arms over his chest, ignoring the hanging questions. "Do you want to explain what the hell is going on Tim?" He asked, his gaze not leaving the smoky posse leaders.

"Aww crap." He stroked a hand through his thick hair, standing it on end.

"Come on, everyone out." Chivvied a small framed woman, pulling and tugging at those reluctant to miss the action, before nodding and taking her exit, closing the wooden door in her wake.

"Okay," Tim stepped forwards, levelling with the broad man. "Con, get that bloody gun outta the guy's face wud ya."

Con snarled, his gaze heating as he spun his wrist hypnotically to Jhonathan's confusion, but as he watched the smoking gun vanished into the air, a shower of thick silvery rain spluttered from its dissipation. Jhonathan ground his teeth. He would not show surprise at the fairy's talents of manifestation. Every fairy was the same to him, well, with the exception of the two writhing in pain at his feet. He would see to it that Shayleigh and Akantha were alright, it was what they had done for him. But after that, he wasn't sure. He wanted his freedom; at any expense.

"Look, take a seat." Tim directed. Jhonathan sat back on the sofa by the heavily wheezing fae who lay still as the dead.

"Come on Con just chill okay." Con took a seat on the edge of the neighbouring sofa, wringing his hands over the fallen fairy's.

Tim stayed standing between them, his attention flitting to the fairy as he spoke. "Look, Ashur didn't want us to say anything yet, but it seems we got no choice." Jhonathan looked him in the eyes.

"We know what's happened to you - k. It's happened to many of us, hell it happened to me. Some of us get more attached to our 'keepers' than others, a kind of Stockholm's syndrome. Others just accept their new reality after escaping. Dude, you ran right home, through the mud and rain and- everything!"

"You were following me?" Jhonathan hadn't realised it was this band of misfits stalking him, he had thought the Queen's guard were hot on his trail. "Why?"

"I don't wanna be the one to tell you this man, but times have changed; literally."

"Literally." Jhonathan drolled.

"Dude you were at your house." He threw his hands in the air "didn't you notice anything?"

Jhonathan slowly shook his head.

"The world's moved on and you noticed nothing." Tim repeated.

"Might as well accept the crap so we can dispose of these fae scum already." Piped in Con, levelling his eyes with Jhonathan's. "That was your ma's house, right? Seems to me the old birds in her 80's now." He smiled viciously as Jhonathan launched across the fairy's to smash his bony fists against Con, instead finding himself held in restraint, his heart and face pounding in tandem.

"No. No! it was a nightmare thanks to the concussion you gave me."

Con lurched forwards on the edge of his sofa. "No, it's the truth." He gritted. "Why do you think so many humans are here among us halflings? You think we want to spend our time running around behind escapees from the fae realm? No, we don't, but we litter pick for the fae so we can fight against them and their obnoxious, power crazy, faemonic Queen!" He threw his hands up in the air standing, and he kicked Shayleigh. Jhonathan stood, facing off with Con as the fairy's body lurched beneath him. Con ground his teeth and he snarled at Jhonathan, before storming from the room, leaving the door to rattle on its hinges. "You fix this crap, Tim, and don't come running to me when it blows up in your face!"

"Great." Tim huffed under his breath before locking eyes with Jhonathan. "It is true. It's all true." He sighed. "None of us wanted it this way but there's nothing we can do about it. Some of us accept it and live here, to fight for the cause, and others leave to go crazy with the knowledge that all they loved has moved on or died. In the end; it's your choice."

Chapter 13

Shayleigh

"Halfling's."

The word ricocheted around Shayleigh's stabilising mind. The image of an angular-faced fairy, hair strung with the plumped vines of summer and whose cosmic blue eyes rippled with watery sadness haunted her mind, waking her from the shock of the poisoned iron.

"Fix this-" The words swam, pulling her from the pain of her injuries, her ears zeroing in on the sound of the unfamiliar voice as she tuned in.

"It's your choice."

"Ha, what choice?" The deadpan voice of her human had her ears twitching in his direction. He wasn't far, but she sensed his turmoil, his heartache, and her magic stirred, longing to soothe it even as she recovered. She didn't know what tethered her to this human's side, but something, just something about his hopeless state had touched her heart.

"Think about it man. Until then, I gotta do sommat about your faemonic friends or Ashur will throw my ass on the streets for endangering the Team.

"Ashur is already here." A dry voice came from the door as it burst open. Blinking, Shayleigh maintained her cover whilst sneaking covert glances at the newcomer.

"Crap." She heard Tim mutter before turning a high voltage smile at the female and purring, "Ashur what a surprise." Teeth clenched, he flicked his wrist glancing at the dark dials of his watch and continued, "you're back early, I thought parents' evening would take longer; did you see Ori's teacher? How's it going with the whole 'see but don't tell' thing?"

Shayleigh listened, curious as she tried to decode the hidden message within, as light footsteps crossed the room, a deep and hungry shadow fell over her.

"This fairy is conscious. Get it back to the cell." Ashur's voice had the silhouette pulsing with growing greed over her form, her heritage shimmering through her pores like the blackest of opals. Shayleigh tried to lurch away from the fairy, but the oppressive shadow swallowed her, its weight laying her body to stone. She could do little more than choke while her magic took its time to flood her veins. But just as suddenly as the fairy attacked, a second shadow befell her, and she gazed up into the earthy brown eyes of Jhonathan.

"She's different." He waved a hand over Akantha whose unconscious body lay not far from her. "Both of them are. They helped me-"

"Escape the fae realm, we know. We know everything that happens with the portals North West of London. And she-" Shayleigh caught sight of Ashur pointing a spiny blackened finger at Akantha's lame body. "She is a pretender. We found our pin on her shirt front, but she is not promised to our cause. Worse than her false identity, she wears the uniform of the fae court; they both do and last I heard the Queen decreed only full blooded fae can work at the palace." She growled. "So don't you," she pointed that charred finger at Jhonathan, "tell me they are saviours and trustworthy. You are no more than a well-loved PET! And you," she turned to Tim. "You-" she seethed, "and I need a serious talk about your elegance. Now move, fae." she commanded, raising her hand.

"You better move man." Tim mumbled to Jhonathan as the shadow grafted itself onto Shayleigh's bones, contorting her sweat soaked skin. But before Jhonathan could shift from his protective crouch over her, she involuntarily lurched upright, cracking their skulls together as he turned in shock to see what was the matter.

"Aaaah." Both groaned. Jhonathan put a hand to his head, whereas Shayleigh still desperately fought the control of Ashur's shadow magic imprisoning her.

"Told yah. Come on," muttered Tim, pulling Jhonathan by the arm from Shayleigh's unresponsive body as the puppet master curled her talons into a fist and yanked her through the possession of her shadow, to her feet.

"Strong thing, aren't you." Ashur purred as she circled Shayleigh before setting her twinkling eyes on hers, her fang tipped smile stretching to her ears in freakish horror. "Maybe I should just put you out of your misery full blood. Or maybe I should make you suffer first." She glanced at Akantha's prone form, raising a dark eyebrow.

Shayleigh fought. Her powers were still recovering from this latest attack, but condensing inside of her ready to erupt in her veins and tunnel from her skin to strike at the evil fairy before her. Moments missed with her powers collecting had Con slamming back through the door to heave Akantha onto his shoulder moaning every vile offence he could think of. Jhonathan and Tim were pressed to the side of the room deep in heated conversation as a second door banged.

Everyone turned to the noise a few meters away. The bubbling sound of voices sprang through the walls with vibrant announcement and Shayleigh smiled internally at the distraction, as she let loose her bolt of magic, which sizzled through her every pour, extinguishing the shadow hold on her in a blaze of burning light.

Screams echoed around her, but Shayleigh couldn't stop the inferno, she didn't dare.

Chapter 14

Akantha

Akantha groaned. Her body was being shocked awake and flooded with power as she fell from a height unknown, her battle instincts kicked in with a deep thudding in her skull. She bent, crouching like a bat, her wings thrust out smacking something hard to her left, the thing she fell from no doubt. She scrunched her vulnerable, tender body in tight, about to beat her leathery pinions as she slammed into the ground, not half as hard as she thought. Panic lit her senses, shooting her eyes open wide to see bolts of high voltage magic being shot through her body from a blinding orb. It was then, she instinctively knew Shay was inside.

A quick scan of the room had her thrust a wing out to coil around Jhonathan, separating him from the humans as she drew him to her side enveloping his feeble frame. "Come-" she hissed, pulling him with her into the light of Shayleigh's orb which stung like a rapid swarm of wasps until her magic recognised them. "Shay, let's get out of here"

"I don't know how!"

"Just walk, the orb will go where you go until your magic depletes itself and deigns to rest. Please, trust me. Mountain fae talk of magic this strong. Trust me - go- hurry!"

Shayleigh stepped forwards, her tail wrapped around her leg and out of harm as Akantha made sure to stay in the eye of the orb or risk drying like a fly sizzling on his lightbulb lover.

With every step, shouts and screams of rage echoed outside of the orb, whereas on the inside all was calm as they exited the room and moved into the long length of the corridor. Quiet sobs racked Shayleigh, her magic exhausted itself with every breath she took.

Akantha was amazed at the strength that Shay held in soul. Never before had she seen a magical orb of such brilliance and wonder. "Holy fae! The orb's down!"

Shayleigh was knocked to the floor, a tall human male standing over her, his head shaved so severely the light from the lamp made it glisten.

He blinked rapidly, his eyes switching from sea blue irises to pits of wholly black awareness that sent the sinewy spines of her pinion shivering as they reactively hid behind her back.

Jhonathan stumbled by her side, no longer bound to her by her wings he stepped forwards, crouched over Shayleigh, his fingers to her throat.

"She's ok," he rumbled. "I told you they just want to protect me -why did you-"

Heavy footsteps halted and a blustering red-faced Ashur pointed out one spindly black finger. "Kill her!" She roared, her shadow puppet raced to do her bidding as a panting Con, along with a crowd of people, all grim faced but determined, caught up to watch the action.

"No."

Akantha shivered. Her mind screamed at her to run, but the warrior inside her had her shaking legs step forwards, her bat-like wings piercing a hole through their terror and coming to slide comfortingly around her friends. She knelt ready to receive the wrath of this unlikely group of comrades. There was no escape from them, not in their mass and with Shayleigh and her new flare of magic out cold, they wouldn't stand a chance. A good warrior always knew when to surrender. It was the time that they had no choices left, only the minimal possibility of being taken as prisoners of war.

"Ashur, non est nostrum modo. Praeterea, ipsa est Princeps." The large male spoke, his eyes gleaming obsidian as he stroked at a long plaid scarf around his caramel neck. Akantha's ears twitched. What the hell were they on about and how did they know the language of the fairy's? Yes, it resembled the human's poetical Latin, but it was not as simple as just speaking it. Their blood language was embedded with magic and its tone emphasised the meaning of the words. So how did a mere mortal, cursed with the sight of Gods and a half blood fairy on a power trip know it?

"In Principem?" Ashur questioned, halting her shadow as it sank into Shayleigh.

"She sure is a princess, bloody full bloods all are. "

"Yeah, Cons right, they all strut around, shoving their magic in people's faces uncaring of any consequences."

"They don't have to care." Tim retorted. "When crap goes down, they get gone and leave us to clean up." He smiled bitterly at Jhonathan, and Akantha knew the two had suffered beneath the rule of the Queen. Her evil spread like a lightning struck tree, harvesting the core to leave only a puppet's shell readily at her command. The open despair inside both males had united them and Akantha could see it even as Jhonathan stood against the crowd, desperate to pull her and Shay limb from limb. Their prejudice all because of an adopted attitude bred into them from birth and an evil Queen whom all, even her court, despised.

"Shut up!" Ashur screamed, turning to the young caramel man as silence swept like a scythe over the crowd. "Ori, what can you see?"

Ori knelt down beside Akantha, a calming glimmer of his blue eyes and a soft touch to her hand resting on Shayleigh's arm comforted her mind. Until the glossy ink blinked into place and a wicked smile signalled the otherworldly awareness was back.

Akantha whipped her hand from beneath his, unwilling to give up her protective position over her friend, as Ori mumbled, "Illa oportet reduceret, quod ipsa perdidit." He blinked, his eyes settling back to calming blue. "She must regain what she has lost." He translated before starting again, "Ea praeterita est key ad futura nostra. Her past is the key to our future."

The crowd leaned closer, everyone silent as Ashur spoke. "Ori, focus hunny." she purred. "What is it exactly that you can see?"

Ori's caramel skinned hand turned pale against Shayleigh's flesh, and she moaned as he began to speak once more. The corridor remained silent as Ori's dark awareness spoke in faemonic rhyme, as they awaited the translation with a touch of hope in their eyes.

"She sits upon the throne, all darkness and greed; those who have escaped her darken her need. But quiet and unseen the Underground Railway goes. Until- wait, no. The vision is changing. I see- I see a beautiful woman with hair of fire, she rests at a Station, a phantom crown upon her head." He let go of Shayleigh and instantly Akantha used a piece of her worn uniform to wipe away the drag of otherworldly plasma from her skin.

"What the hell does that mean?" A young woman piped up.

"It means-" Tim started

"We kill her!" Con roared, excited hollering's took up his battle call as he pushed through the few who dared to conceal his view, ramming a shoulder in here, and trampling a foot there. Then voices raged and Jhonathan slipped from Akantha's protection, body checking the fuming Con, face to face, their noses touching as they spat insults. Then suddenly Ashur's shadow was upon him, suspending his motion as the grinding of his teeth echoed around the silent corridor. Jhonathan froze at the warning glare in her eyes before Tim toed him into the crowd and away from sight.

Akantha wondered what horror awaited them as Shayleigh began to moan and wither as she slowly regained consciousness.

Chapter 15

Jhonathan

Jhonathan watched from behind a mountain of leather clad shoulders. Tim had tried to pull him from the room completely, but this time he had had enough, and shirked from his grip. Standing his ground, his heart racing; expecting a painful retaliation, but none came. His first victory in years and he had done it to find out the fate of the fairy's he thought would never mean anything more than an escape ticket to him.

Tim now stood beside him, shoulder to shoulder, as they watched Shayleigh stir from her pillow of afro curls beneath the authoritarian Ashur. A sweat that had nothing to do with his own predicament broke free of his skin, confusing his hidden heart that had been put in lockdown under the

Queen's rule. Now it was breaking free of its restraints, beating a little faster at the sound of her voice as she cocked her head to one side, raised an aristocratic brow and questioned her captor, "What do you want with us?"

Jhonathan could practically smell the hatred that rose from the tall woman. That was obviously why she had magic, but the animosity spreading across her overcasting brows was fit to strike even without the storm brewing in her glassy obsidian eyes. Like everyone else in this so-called hostel, she too, wore the black leather outfit more befitting a fighting arena than a place that took in strays.

The crowds' mumblings ceased at the rise of Cons girthy palm. Ashur sucked hard on her bottom lip, revealing two brilliant white fangs.

"What the hell is she?" He hissed, turning to glance at Tim who without moving replied. "Ashur, our leader, our saviour, a Halfling."

"Halfling." Jhonathan turned the word over in his mouth.

"Yes, part fairy and part human."

"Oh my God, who in hell would willingly conceive with the fairy's?" He spoke too soon for his brain to churn the thought over. "Oh God, the Queen."

Tim nodded slowly and a sickening lump formed in Jhonathan's throat. He had thought the Queen was evil in physical brutality and leadership, not a power-crazy fairy bent on creating half-breeds. But then that didn't fit. Something wasn't right.

"Why?" He asked, watching an Ashur flipped her green rooted hair, dulled with black tips before she leaned down to Shayleigh.

"Why else? Power."

"But the palace houses only pure-blooded fairy and none of them would touch a human, let alone- "

"And you know all the secrets of the Seelie Queen?" Tim retorted as a stout woman shushed them from in front of the crowd.

Jhonathan quieted his mouth, but he could not squash the thoughts swimming around his head at the speed of lightning, birthing all kinds of horrific tortures the Seelie Queen could unleash upon them.

From his viewing point at the back of the crowd Jhonathan watched as Ashur plastered a kind smile to her abrasive face, the tips of her fangs almost puncturing her thickened bottom lip as she reached her hand down and offered it to Shayleigh.

Jhonathan held his breath as Shayleigh turned to Akantha, a look passed between them before she reached out and clasped the offered hand, allowing Ashur to flick her fingers and snap her shadow magic back up before pulling Shayleigh to her shaky feet. The leader turned to the mass of people, eyeing each of them; including himself, giving him a single raised eyebrow, which sent shivers down his spine.

"I Ashur De'Bront stand before you as my witnesses upon this day, this hour, I accept the full-blooded fairy's before me into our station; our hostel. Let it be known, that none here, not now or ever may revoke the hospitality I offer these two."

"There you go," Tim chuckled amid the begrudging crowd mumbling their welcomes. "We're all good now, you and the fairy's get to stay."

Giving a sideways tilt to his mouth Jhonathan ignored Tim's prattling, straining to hear what was being said by the leader, Ashur.

"From now on, you are one of us, you and your friend." She spoke sincerely through words that cracked like a whip with their ferocity. But the fairy's seemed to be unaffected, in fact, as he watched Akantha, he noticed her shoulders relax, the tension falling from her wings as the words were spoken. "There are rules of course- but for now let's just get you cleaned up. And out of those- that uniform."

"What about Jhonathan?" Shayleigh asked, searching the thinning crowd until their eyes locked. She tilted her head in that weird way of hers, blinking unnaturally with her side eyelids. He quirked the opposite side of his mouth up before tracing it with his hardened fingertips. This was the first time he had smiled in what felt like ages. The very first time he had smiled at a fairy and suddenly his heart softened.

"-fine." He tuned back in, just as Tim grabbed his arm and ploughed him through the remaining crowd.

"Come on, boss says you stink." He chuckled.

"And how did you hear that when I didn't?" Jhonathan asked, only half joking.

"Look man, you gotta get cleaned up or this whole pad's gonna reek!" He spared a fleeting glance at his wrist and tutted. "Better hurry too, it's night and that means Con's cooking, so it's burgers all around." He smiled as they sped past the man himself. "Aye Con?!" He teased as they hurried down the corridor to Cons barely legible mutter.

"Yeah, fae burgers."

Chapter 16

Akantha

Akantha knew something was dodgy when the shadow wielding fairy offered her hand to Shayleigh. The whole situation with the creepy boy, Ori, proved that this group of misfits were up to more than just keeping low profiles in case the fairy Queen stumbled upon them. Their situation was dire and their only option was the offer of friendship born of deceit via the leader; Ashur.

But true to her word the Halfling leader had allowed them to bathe, offered them clean clothing, which although rather small seemed to fit enough for their human glamours to appear 'normal', if black leather was what they saw as the height of fashion. Although the conniving leader had offered Shayleigh a silken blouse of forest green, no battle garments for her and strangely enough the whole outfit fit as if it was made for her despite her deformities.

Unsurprisingly, Ashur had adopted her place at Shayleigh's side. Her heart raged its anger, feeding her soul full of magic, daring her to go dark. This whole situation smelt like dragon dung to her. But what could she do about it? The Halfling was usurping a position to which she would undoubtedly use to gain Shayleigh's ear. But she didn't know Shay as Akantha did. And one way or another the bitch would slip up and Akantha would be there to see her downfall and scatter her ashes.

So, for now, she would continue to have her best friend's back, literally and otherwise, as she investigated the possible advantages Ashur would gain from befriending Shayleigh. As she worked on her battle strategy; to escape, reopen the portal, and return home. Praying to all thing's fairy, that the Queen had not noticed their absence. For if she did, they were as good as dead fairy's walking.

They walked the long corridors and into the lounge they had earlier fallen through the wall in. Inside, amongst a scattering of oddly mismatched cushions Akantha spotted Jhonathan's, brows deep over angry swirling irises as he glared at the half blood; Con, opposite him. She made a mental note to find out what was going on there, for Shay would be heartbroken if anything bad befell the human.

Suddenly her stomach growled and the room's occupants turned towards her in laughter.

"Enough!" Ashur demanded, taking Akantha's arm as she gently guided her arm, pointing out her office where Shayleigh, dressed in forest green, her hair bleeding down it. She sat munching on human food. "We will eat in my office today." Ashur announced, throwing a silent look of disapproval over her shoulder into the room of relaxing people before shutting her office door with a loud clunk. She smiled strenuously and indicated a squishy cube for Akantha to sit on while she practically ignored her for the rest of their meal.

It was okay, Akantha assured herself, as she looked up from her lowered position in the corner of the room. Ashur thought she was in charge, she thought she had Shay's ear, but nothing, nothing would come between the years of friendship they shared and no one could out strategize a mountain fairy. Especially not a half-breed with the freaky throwback magic of a full-blooded fairy.

Akantha chewed on her food until it was a tasteless pulp, churning the reasoning for Ashur's shift in her mind over and over again, her heart thumping a rain dance in her chest. The most frustrating part was that she was sure this whole 'I'm a nice halfling' act had something to do with the young man Ori and what he had said to Ashur.

But Akantha had been so full of terror at the otherworldly entity resting in his eyes she had not heard what he spoke, just the whispered message that entered her mind through the creature's telekinesis. The message of vengeance.

But vengeance for what and why? She feared she would not know the answer until it was too late. She feared the entity it came from, but most disturbing of all was the fact that she feared the human host Ori.

"Well, I think it's about time we made it official." Ashur barked, drawing Akantha out of her musings of her own admissions of weakness. She held out a hand to Shayleigh and Akantha craned her neck to see the small slate badge speckled with silver and the letters P.E.T carved inside. Shay smiled, a hint of fang peeking through her glamour as she pinned it to her green blouse, before turning to Akantha with a big grin decorating her face, her tail tip flicking over her shoulder like a contented cat.

Ashur faced her, but not with a badge in her palm nor smile on her lips. No, the snarl she gave Akantha was cold and cruel, full of calculated vengeance as she snipped "I would give you one, but you already wear the one I bestowed on Zaran." Her eyes darkened, her shadow puppet leached free of her hold and danced its way to Akantha's body, its touch as cold and yet scolding as ice before it was whipped away, back under the control of its master. "That pin is a special one. It radiates his lucky magic. I suggest you wear it; you're gonna need all the luck you can get." She stated dryly before turning back to Shayleigh and opening her arms wide;

"I officially welcome you to the Pet Empathiser Team!"

- The End; for now –

Pronunciation

Jhonathan (silent h)

Akantha
(ah-can-tha)

Shayleigh
(Sh-ahy-lee)

Seya
(say-ah)

Lord Coimagnus's
(co-ey-magnus)

Printed in Great Britain
by Amazon